Chapter 1:

The four teenaged boys parked their small truck in front of the old rundown house on the outskirts of town and made their way up the dirt driveway. Their only light was the moon that shone bright that Halloween night, as they approached the house; no street lights were out this far. At the bottom of the porch steps, they paused. One of the boys pulled out his cellphone. He snapped a picture of the house and then started a live video feed as they walked up the old steps.

The Halloween party that they had been at prior to driving almost out of town to the old house, was at one of the more popular student's houses. They overheard someone telling a campfire horror story and sat down to listen. When the story was done, they all laughed. All four of them assumed the story was nothing more than a story. The young man telling the story dared them to prove him wrong and as cocky as they thought they were, they accepted. Neither one of them believed in ghosts anyways, so it seemed like a fun thing to do on a Friday night. Someone wrote the address down, told them the rules and they left.

Arrogantly thinking that the house was not haunted, they opened the door and stepped inside. Using their cellphones as flashlights, they stepped into the entryway. The entryway was covered in cobwebs and had broken floorboards and holes in the plaster with the wooden lath exposed through most of the holes. A staircase was to their right with half of the banister missing at the top, even a few stairs. They went right into the room and stepped further into the house. Other than some old, dusty and broken furniture, it was pretty much the same. Some of the bricks from the fireplace had fallen and lay scattered on the old rotting wooden mantle and on the hearth. Windows were broken with tattered curtains hanging in them. There were signs that animals were living in the house or had at one time. Animals had made what looked like nests in the couch and the corner by the window closest to the fireplace.

The dining room looked a lot like the living room; broken windows and only scraps of furniture. The only use left for that furniture was as firewood. The floor boards creaked as they walked into the kitchen, scanning the phone around the room to appease their live audience on the other end.

Cupboards had doors missing. Some were broken and had parts of the countertop falling into them. The refrigerator door was missing, along with the range, and only the pipes were visible from where the sink used to be. Part of the kitchen floor was missing, and they could see some 2X4's showing through. Looking down through the floor, they could see into the dirt basement with help from the camera light on the phone. The door to the back was barely being held up by the hinges; pulled wrong and it would fall.

"Did you hear that?" asked Toby, one of the young men.

"Wind," replied the red haired boy, named Brian.

"No, that," said Toby.

They all stopped walking and listened. There was the faint sound of tapping coming from above their heads. They headed to the staircase to investigate the sound.

"How are we supposed to get up there?" asked a blond boy named Michael.

"If we stay close to the wall, we should be able to get past the missing boards and rails on the stairs," said Brian.

The tapping sound sounded closer and they moved faster on the stairs, hugging the wall continuing climbing. Adam, another blond boy who oversaw the live feed, was the last one up. At the top of the stairs, they listened again for the tapping sound. The sound was coming from the right. They headed in that direction. As they got to the end of the hall, there was a door. The tapping sound was coming from the other side of the door.

"Ok, here goes nothing," said Brian, pushing Adam to the front of the group. "Camera guy goes in first."

Adam opened the door and was shoved through by his friends. They followed very close. The wind blew the door shut behind them. They jumped and turned around. They jumped again when they heard tapping right behind them. A dark figure crawled towards them.

"AAAAAHHHHHHHH," they all screamed.

"Run," yelled Brian. They turned to run but were met with another dark figure crawling toward them.

"There is nowhere to go," cried Michael.

The dark figures started laughing. They stood up and another boy came out of the closet holding another camera, laughing like crazy.

"One of them peed their pants," laughed Jackson, the storyteller and the one who dared the boys.

"You are going to post this?" asked Brian.

"And the one you guys made too."

"You are jerks, total jerks," said Adam. "But we were right. This house is not haunted; the story you told us was bogus. There are no ghosts in this house, no murder, no disappearance. Nothing happened, we completed the dare. You lose, we win."

"It doesn't matter. This is still going on the internet and it's gonna go viral," laughed Robert.

"Let's go guys," said Michael. He pushed one of the boys dressed in dark out of his way and reached for the door knob. It started turning by itself. Scratching came from the other side of the door. "Funny. When are you going to stop?"

"Whatever. Trying to scare us now," laughed Jackson stepping forward to open the door. He froze, when he saw the door knob turning, like someone was trying to get into a locked room. The scratching got louder and sounded like it was behind them. He turned around, and went pale. His eyes got huge and he looked terrified and his pants were now wet also. The rest of the boys laughed, thinking this was part of the joke too. When they turned around they saw a grayish figure squatting on the ceiling. Gray legs and arms looked like skin covering bones. It reached for them with its gray skin covered fingers that had black holes where the fingernails should have been. They looked like whatever it was had been scratching something until its fingernails fell off. Its black, stringy, greasy hair hugged tight to its head as if it was not upside down at all. It dropped from the ceiling to the floor, spinning so that it landed on its feet and slowly stood. Walking slowly towards the boys, it dragged one leg and one arm hung low on the same side. The eye sockets were black. Black goo covered the ears, nose and dripped from the mouth as it made an eerie screechy scream that sounded vaguely like an animal being killed. There were also what looked like chunks of its flesh missing, like something had taken a bite out of the creature. Black goo covered the bite marks as well, along with scratches. It reached towards the boys and moved in spurts of lightning fast speed between slow dragging steps.

The boys screamed and rushed toward the door. They flung it open to find another creature on the other side of the door. It grabbed Jackson and opened its mouth and bit him on the neck. It swallowed the flesh and muscle as Jackson fell to the ground holding his neck, blood gushing out between his fingers. He was dead before he hit the floor. More of the creatures jumped on him, ripping at him like he was a roasted chicken and they hadn't eaten in months. Two of them tore at his intestines and internal organs, with more pulling pieces of him off or grabbing the pieces thrown about and scurrying away with their prize.

More creatures pushed themselves into the room, coming from the door, side, bottom and ceiling, scratching and reaching for the boys. Some crawled and some shuffled, but they were lightning fast, not like the one already in the room. As if the smell of blood and given them speed. It seemed like they would never stop coming inside. Soon the room was overflowing with these things.

The remaining boys ran for the windows trying to avoid the hands reaching for them, using what broken furniture was there to fight them off. Adam got the window opened, and fell out as the other boys pushed at him to get to the window first. There was no ledge or anything to grab onto so all he could do was fall and hope he didn't die also. He landed hard on a stone bench that was just below the window in a little garden at that side of the house. The sound of bones breaking was followed with a sharp pain and then no pain anywhere in his back or legs. He tried to get his legs to move, but nothing-they would not respond to his brain telling them to get up and run. Reaching to touch his legs, he could feel them with his fingers, but no feeling of his fingers on his legs. Paralyzed, there was nothing he could do. No escape. He could hear the other boys screaming and a few he could see try to get out the window, but getting yanked back in. He tried to reach his phone, but it had fallen further away than he was able to reach without his legs. It was probably broken in the fall anyway.

Soon there was no noise coming from the open window. Tears rolled down his face as he was sure what had happened to his friends and the other boys. Adam lay there on the stone bench trying to will his legs to move or to just get off the bench, for he feared the same fate if he could not make his now useless legs work.

He heard a shuffling noise coming from the front of the house. The creatures now covered in blood banged on the glass of the window that was a few feet from where the bench was. They wanted him also, so they screeched in frustration. The shuffling sound grew closer and his legs were lifted as he was pulled off the bench. His head slammed to the ground and a sharp white light blinded him temporarily. Something was pulling him back into the house, up the front steps and through the front door. He lifted his head to try to see what had him and to avoid hitting every step with the back of his already sore head. He heard his shoes clunk onto the floor as his legs were dropped, just inside the entryway of the house. The creatures rushed at him in a crazy frenzy, in lightning fast movements. Glad to have no feeling in his lower half of his body, he watched the things fight over one of his legs.

The one that seemed to be the leader from the room upstairs made a noise and the rest backed off. Adam felt himself being dragged again, into the kitchen, his body falling into the open holes in the floor and then being yanked out. He started screaming, yelling for help hoping one of the boys had gotten away. No one came. As his head hit every step on the way down to the basement there was no pain; he knew he was dying. He was getting weak and very tired.

Adam forced himself to look around the dark basement through the black spots in his eyes. His eyes adjusted to the dark and with the help of the little moonlight coming in from the kitchen above, he could make out the remains of the other boys. The creatures were still feasting on them. New creatures from somewhere in the basement crawled towards him.

They took chunks out of his body and ripped into his body cavity. Reaching inside his stomach, they pulled out intestines and other internal organs. Blood was pouring out of his mouth and he was starting to drown in his own blood.

Adam could feel his life fading away. They ripped open his chest, his lungs too full of blood for him to scream, he just cried silently. For the brief seconds before he died, he saw the leader rip out his heart and take a bite.

His last thought was hoping he was on his way to Heaven and not Hell to relive this nightmare every day. He felt the tears and blood running down his face. And finally, nothing.

Chapter 2:

"The missing boys are now feared dead after rescue teams searched for days in the house and the surrounding fields, lakes and rivers. According to other teenagers at the party, one of the missing three older boys dared the younger boys to go visit the old house on Bremerton Ave. They were planning on scaring the four boys in a prank. The police and sheriff have checked the house several times and still have not found any evidence of any of the boys actually being in the house. Though their cars were found parked in front and hidden in the back, there is no other sign of them ever being there. They were reported to have been streaming live to prove that they went into the house, but no video has been found," said the news reporter live from the Michaels house.

"Some of the town people told us stories about the house being haunted and other stories about the property surrounding the house. We checked the public records department and police records and there is nothing to confirm any of the stories. We did find that the original owners and builders of the house were Ryan and Katarina Michaels. Though in 1984 there were reports of someone living in the house, with further investigation, these reports were also found to be unsubstantiated," reported the reporter. The cameraman scanned the surrounding area with his camera for some extra footage for the news that night. The camera showed the fire trucks, police cars, ambulances, sheriff's cars and many volunteers and onlookers surrounding the front of the house and the officials going in and out of the house.

The house had always been a topic of conversation in town in years past, but as the town grew the story stopped being told. If there was any truth to any of the stories, those that knew the truth rarely talked about it anymore and never to media or law enforcement. There were some older folks that would talk about it but only on rare occasions. With this recent missing persons' investigation, the local paper printed the story of the house and the family that lived there and the stories told throughout the years.

"The house was built in 1880 in Lewiston Heights, Montana by Ryan Michaels, who had inherited a gold mine at 18 from his parents and made his fortune after several big hits of gold before he was 20. He grew up local and poor. His parents were Jeanette and

Robert Michaels, who died from influenza when Ryan, their only child, turned 18. Robert inherited the mine from his father, but was always too poor to attempt to search for the gold said to be in the mine.

Ryan Michaels, became very stingy with his money, rarely paying for anything and had even refused to pay the men who built his house the price they had agreed on. He was the type that changed his mind after something was done, argue that it was not to his specifications and demand a discount. Most would not argue with him. It was just easier to let him have his way. At the time he had a lot of clout in the town, especially since he had more money than anyone combined in town and could make or break any business, just by saying anything. He did not even trust banks; he kept his money hidden somewhere in the house, as the story went.

His wife, Katarina, was young and from Europe. He traveled there in 1900 at 38 and came back with a wife who was 20 years younger than him and worshiped the ground he walked on. She came from a very poor family and townspeople said she was bought from her family making them very wealthy where they lived. Others said he stole her because he was too cheap to pay for anything, let alone a beautiful young woman to be his wife. She was very nice to everyone, but blinded by love or gratitude. She never spoke out against her husband; waited on him hand and foot. People said she was more of a maid then a wife, but she seemed happy. After they had children, her feelings for her husband changed. She finally saw him for who he really was. Mean, cranky, stingy and cruel.

They had four children, two boys and two girls, by the time she was 21. Jonathon, Thomas, Meredith and Amelia all looked a lot like their mother, with olive skin, dark hair and bright green eyes. Nothing like their father with his grayish hair, gray eyes and gray skin. The girls were friendly and caring and very outgoing, like their mother. They married young to young men in town, while the boys, personalities like their father, waited until they were a bit older and traveled to Europe and brought back wives.

Jonathon and Thomas anticipated taking over the family business and building homes on the property to raise their families. Katarina's daughters were disowned for marrying farmers and not the older gentlemen their father had picked out for them. Though Katarina missed them, she knew they would be happier with true love. She thought she found it in Ryan, but after years with him, she knew it was more gratitude for rescuing her from her poor life.

Ryan died in his sleep at the age of 54 in 1916, still having the first dollar he ever made. Because she was a woman, her husband had left her nothing. The house, mine and money was left to their sons and their wives. Katarina died several years after him at 51 in 1933, after a long illness that set on soon after he died. Four years after Katarina died, Jonathon's wife died in childbirth along with their only child, a boy. Thomas and his wife were killed by some strange illness a 2 years after that. They had no children. Meredith, her husband and their children also died that same year from the same illness. Amelia and her family survived the illness only to die in a mysterious fire at their farm one night about 3 years later.

Jonathon died alone and in the house, searching for the money. No one really knows when. In 1948, all that was found was his corpse that had been lying there for a very long time. There were teeth marks on the bones and bones scattered all through the house, like wild animals had him for dinner over the months it took for him to completely decompose.

The money was never found and the house remained empty for many, many years. With no other living heirs, the house and property became county owned, yet no one wanted to live in the house, especially with all the stories about shadows being seen from the windows late at night. In early 1970's a developer came to town and was interested in the property. He wanted to tear down the house and build an exclusive resort for people to come and hunt or enjoy an adventure-something high class people from the cities would gladly pay a lot for. The house was very close to a river for boat rides and there were mountains for hiking and lots of wildlife for hunting. The sale was almost final when the developer disappeared.

It was said that he had heard all the legends about the house being haunted and did not believe in any of that "hocus-pocus" junk. Everyone heard the stories about the creatures and would not step foot on the property, let alone in the house. After several crews quit before even starting the work, he decided to prove to all of them that the stories were made up.

He called the local newspaper and had them write a story about his endeavor to spend the night and possibly part of his stay in the house and on the property. He hoped by sleeping there, he could prove that the house and land were safe. The reporter met him at the house in the early evening and went through the house with him. Just as the sun set, the reporter left, and the developer went into the house for the night with two of his employees, both of whom volunteered to go.

The next morning, when the reporter arrived he waited and waited for them to come out, but nothing. After searching himself, he headed back into town to get the sheriff to search the house more thoroughly. The sheriff came up with no sign that the developer and his group had ever been there. Checking with the developer's office, his secretary had not heard from him at all. The search lasted weeks, but nothing was ever found of any of them. No bodies, no sign they were ever there at all. Nothing.

Over the years the house had fallen apart from age and weather. Townspeople had spent years trying to get the house demolished. It was always approved, but no company would ever do the job, not even from other towns. The surrounding property was sold off to developers except for the 1 acre fenced around the house, but it all sat unused, with no one wanting to be on the sold land until the house was demolished.

Chapter 3:

"The television show Haunted House Debunkers is in town this week to investigate the old Michaels home. They have heard the stories of the house and it piqued their interest, especially with the most recent new report. With their investigation, they hope to tell us what happened to the boys and to debunk the haunting," said the local news reporter. "The plan is to spend the night in the house a few nights and later to have answers for us. The parents of the missing boys are praying that they can have some closure and possible answers."

The Haunted House Debunkers' lead investigator, Robert Smith, checked the feed for the inside cameras with their main IT guy, James Monroe. Normally they only ran about 5 cameras equipped with night vision, but because this house was so large and each room had no viewpoint to the other, they were running around 15 cameras. Plus, there were twice the motion detectors and a few full-spectrum cameras throughout the house. Everyone would be carrying EMF and EVP recorders. They had even brought in a few extra investigators from their normal 4 regulars on the show.

Robert Smith stood outside the large house and took it all in. It was a large old mansion, with wood slats covering the outside of the house with shutters on the outside of every window. The porch wrapped completely around the front of the house and both sides. There were pieces of the outside walls that were missing and most of the shutters were barely hanging on. The roof was old wooden shingles and was missing large sections that either had holes into the attic or the lath wood roof was exposed. Stepping onto the porch, he avoided the broken steps and rails to open the front door and step inside. This was the first time he had entered the house since they got there two days ago.

There were cobwebs, broken floorboards, holes in the plaster with the wooden lath exposed throughout the entry way and the rest of the rooms he could see. The staircase had half of the bannister missing at the top, even a few stairs. Stepping further into the house he saw broken furniture, animal feces, broken glass, leaves and branches. The wood floor that remained was stained and curled up wherever the outside elements breached the holes in the roof and broken windows. Mother Nature and local townspeople were not kind to this old house. With the rocks in the rooms close to the broken windows, it looked to him like the windows had a little help getting broke.

Upstairs he could hear Yoh, walking around checking equipment. Robert stopped for a moment and listened. He thought he heard something dragging behind him. He turned and went back into the living room, looking for the source of the sound. There was nothing. He ruled it out to be a raccoon or another animal in the walls. He could hear tires coming from outside on the driveway, so he left the house.

Their research analyst, Amanda, had been at the public library, the records office in town and had traveled to the county seat to check there. She planned to dig up any and all information about the house and its history including, hopefully, blueprints. Her ability to get people who did not want to talk to spill their guts, had them looking forward to getting some interesting local lore on the house.

"I am gonna guess by that smile, you have something for us," laughed Robert. "What did you find?"

"Tons. Did you know that there are more than 25 missing case files that surround this house? Supposedly, the 30 or so people who have been reported missing in the last 20 years all were heading here to either complete a dare or were just interested in seeing if this house was haunted. Some of the older residents hinted that this land was stolen Indian land. Others say that this land is cursed, not sure as to why, but nothing has ever grown here at all. One man said the house is built on an old satanic worship site. Nevertheless, there are a lot of missing people reports associated with this house and land. And a lot of other even weirder stories."

"That's great," said Robert. Jessica Flynn, Darlene Mitchel and Donavan McHale, from the American Network show, walked over to where they were and listened. Hunter Starter, McKenna Wright and Ryan Martins from their European based show, put down their equipment and headed to them. Yoh Lee was still in the house running equipment checks.

"The history of the owners of the house is exactly as the paper printed. So were the histories of the family members and how they died. I did hear that people say that Jonathon, the last Michaels, was so mad that he could not find the money that he had a gypsy curse put on the house so that no one else could find the missing money."

"How much money are we talking about?" asked Hunter.

"Roughly around $750,000. That was a fortune in the time that the Michaels lived. Supposedly he never spent a dime and hid the money in the house. When he died he never told his sons where the money was. Even if they found it, they never would have been able to spend it all. They all died within 30 years of their father dying."

"Is it a finder's keepers sort of situation? If we find it, we keep it?" asked Hunter.

"Pretty much. Though I really want to find out what is going on with this house. Who cares about the money? Did you know Jonathon was found dead in the house and that they actually have no idea how long he had been dead?"

"Weird," said McKenna. "Not sure what to believe."

"Well something happened to those boys and the other people," said James. "Plus stories change over the years and an old house is almost always the center of stories and rumors. For all we know there could be a serial killer in town and he has been kidnapping people, killing them and covering it up."

"If that were true, he or she would be almost 100 years old, because I doubt they started killing people as an infant," said Robert. "There is something about this house and whatever it is, I hope we catch it on tape."

"Speaking of tape, I need to start checking the equipment in the van. I need you guys inside to do sound and video checks and fix anything that needs to be fixed before we start tonight," James said, heading to the van. Robert followed with Amanda on his heels with all her notes and reports. The rest of the team members headed into the house, ready to run the tests.

James starting checking the camera feeds, when he noticed Yoh, inside the house setting up some of the last minute equipment, waving at the camera. He was looking excited as he jumped up and down pointing at his headset.

Switching on the microphone, they could hear the excitement in his voice "Get in here! I got something. Get in here now," he yelled.

"On my way," answered Robert. "Have Hunter and McKenna meet us, too."

"Done."

Robert entered the house, just as Hunter and McKenna come into the entry from the kitchen and together they ran up the stairs. Yoh had on earphones and was listening to the recorder when they got into the room. He had an intense look of seriousness on his face and kept rewinding and replaying whatever was on the tape.

"What's up Yoh?" asked Robert.

"This better be good. We were still trying to get equipment set up in the kitchen," said Hunter.

"Listen to this." Yoh took off the headphones and passed them to Robert. His eyes got huge and he started to smile. He passed them off to Hunter who listened and gave them to McKenna. They all were smiling and couldn't believe what they had heard.

"Was that what I thought it was?" McKenna asked.

"What did you hear," asked Yoh. He heard something and wanted to make sure they heard the same thing.

"I heard a voice," said Robert. "Hard to make out what it said."

"Sounded to me like an 'A' name," answered Hunter. "Are you sure there was no interference or that someone wasn't playing a prank on you? No cross talk from the mics?"

"I was doing a sound check and when I played it back, there is was," explained Yoh. "I even ran back the camera and there was no one in the room or by the door."

"We need to get Jennifer in here and see what she senses," said Robert.

Before they could radio James to send her up, she walked into the room.

"Got a feeling you might need me," she said. They had met Jennifer a few years ago during an investigation. She was a well-known psychic in her area, but they believed that she was a phony. She was on several different episodes until they were convinced that she was not faking. When Robert called, she jumped at the opportunity to help them out in Montana. She had been wandering around the house trying to see if she could feel anything or anyone, when she got the feeling they needed her upstairs.

"Yoh was running a sound check and got something on the EVP. Have you sensed anything that we need to focus on or be worried about?" asked Robert.

"There's more than one, a few actually. Curious, though, as to why we are here. Very curious," she said walking around the room. "They have been watching us and staying close to wherever we are. This is their house and they want to be sure we aren't here to destroy it. I think it is Ryan Michaels and his family."

"Do you think that we will be safe tonight?" asked McKenna. "Are we in any danger?"

"No, these spirits are just curious and I doubt they will do anything to scare us intentionally. Besides spirits do not have a form, they are just an energy. They can't hurt your or touch you because they do not have a physical form and energy cannot hurt you. The touching and being physically hurt is just for Hollywood. They use their energy in different ways to try to communicate or let you know they are here. But for most purposes they are just observing us. Completely harmless. I do think they will participate with your search tonight. You may be surprised at what you get."

"What about poltergeists?" asked Hunter. "There are documented cases where they move objects and hurt people."

"That is negative energy. Harmless also, even though it is negative. Besides, anyone can Photoshop anything these days. If you look carefully at those videos, they can all be explained and proven fake. You've seen the video about the car crashes where you can't see the other car they hit? All Photoshop or some other fancy computer program."

There was a loud bang as the door to the room closed suddenly as a breeze blew in from the open window. They all jumped and then started laughing nervously. The thought of some energy watching them was creepy, but if it had watched what happen to the boys, they might get some answers tonight. There was only a few minutes left until sunset and still a lot of set up to do.

"Let's get the equipment set up and check finished," suggested Robert. "I am looking forward to tonight's investigation. I have a feeling we might find out what happened to those boys. This may be our best episode yet."

"What if we don't like the answer," said McKenna with a shudder. She looked from face to face of her fellow investigators and saw the same thing, excitement and worry.

Chapter 4

The rest of the team headed back to where they had come from, and Jennifer stayed behind. She wanted to see if she could feel anything else in the room now that the rest of the crew had left. Sitting in a folding chair that Yoh had left, she listened to the quiet. There had been a very faint voice that was tickling the back of her mind since she got to the house. Even in all the silence, it was hard to make out what it was saying, but she knew it was young, possibly one of the missing boys. Every time she was almost able to hear, another voice came and quieted it. There were many voices talking but the quiet one was who she was trying to hear. The other voices sounded old, like they had been around for a very long time. Possibly before the house was even built.

"I can barely hear you," said Jennifer. "Slow down and concentrate harder. I want to hear what you are saying."

She closed her eyes again and listened harder. Eyes shot open and she suddenly felt very scared. She stood up and ran to the door, just as it slammed shut. She felt surrounded and fear overcame her. It felt as if spirits were pushing against her in a crowded elevator.

Just as she thought she was going to suffocate, it stopped. The door opened by itself and she ran downstairs, stopping at the bottom to calm down and relax. They were gone. Whatever they were, they had left her when she left the room.

In all her years as a psychic, she had never felt anything that evil. Like the spirits upstairs meant to harm them tonight. It only took her a moment to realize what had happened to those boys. The voice at the outskirts of her mind was very loud. It warned her to leave and not come back. The house wanted them. The curious impression was just their way of playing with her and getting her to let her guard down. She told the rest of the crew not to worry, and she needed to let them know, they needed to cancel the investigation. They needed to do more research about the house and the property.

She reached for the door as the feeling of being surrounded came at her again. She fumbled with the door got it open, but it slammed shut. She tried the knob again, but it was locked. She felt more of the same coming at her and the feel of evil was overwhelming her and scaring her. Invisible hands grabbed her tried to pull her back upstairs, their touch was like ice and very strong. She needed to get out and warn the others. The investigation needed to be stopped. She fought hard against the hands and managed to break free.

She ran to the closest window and looked to see if anyone was close enough to hear her yell. Robert was by the study outside, setting up outside cameras. She ran to the study, the door was open and she ran in. Before she made it to the door, she caught an image in the broken mirror at the end of the hall to her right. It looked like a young boy in ripped up clothes, covered in blood. His eyes were hollow and he looked like he was waving her over. She walked towards the mirror. As she got close, a grayish figure limped out of the shadows in the corner and reached for her. Grey skin covered bones made it look like a walking skeleton with black goo coming from open bite marks and scratches all over its body. Its hands looked sinister with black holes where the fingernails should have been, reached at her and came within inches of her. Hollow, black eyes stared at her with black goo leaking from its mouth, nose and ears. Matted, black stringy hair covered its head and part of its face.

Quickly she stepped away from his grasp, only to bump into more of the creatures. She turned and was grabbed by the one from the corner. Gathering up all her courage, she ran and pushed her way through the creatures that were slowly gathering around her. One grabbed her ankle causing her to fall and she tried to push her way through. She scrambled to her feet and ran into the study and slammed the door.

"Robert! Get me out of here!" she screamed, banging on the window. Robert looked up. She was hoping she could break the window, but it would not. The glass held no matter how hard she pounded on it.

The scared look on her face shocked him into dropping what he held and rush to the door.

He called Hunter and Yoh for help. Together they made it to the door and tried to open it. They could get it open a few inches and it would slam shut. Jennifer was on the other side trying to help the best that she could.

She could hear the shuffling as the creatures moved closer and closer to her. She screamed and pulled at the door. It would not budge.

"Get the crowbar," said Hunter. Yoh ran off to get it, while Robert and Hunter rammed themselves into the door, trying to break it down. It was like the door was being held shut by someone or something. No matter how hard they rammed it, the door would not move more than half an inch or so. Yoh came back with crowbar and rammed it in between the door and door jam. With all three of them, they were able to get the door open and held it open long enough for Jennifer to get out. The door slammed shut as they pulled her onto the porch.

"What the hell happened?" asked Robert.

"I have no idea what happened. You left and this evil feeling entered the room. It was like I was being suffocated and squeezed- I couldn't breathe or scream. After I made it downstairs, there was a reflection in the mirror next to the bathroom that caught my eye. I swear it was one of the missing boys. When I went to check, there was something that reached for me from the shadows. Like something from every nightmare I have ever had. Then there were more. It was the worst thing I have ever felt, plus when it reached for me one actually was able to grab my ankle."

The door swung open and Robert stepped in, holding the door open and looked around. There was nothing there. Jennifer bravely stepped back in and looked around.

"There is nothing here," said Robert. "Are you sure you saw something?"

"I know I saw something in the mirror. The spirit could have made me think I saw the things and felt them. But there is something evil in there," Jennifer said backing out of the house.

Robert followed her out and shut the door. They all stood on the porch and looked concerned. Do they believe her and cancel the investigation or do they just chalk it up to psychic mumbo jumbo? Some of them still did not believe that she was really psychic. For some it was an easy decision, the rest were still on the fence.

"You said they can't hurt us," said Hunter.

"What I felt and saw or think I did, looked like it could."

"What did it look like?" asked Yoh.

"Like something from hell that crawled out of the every one of Wes Craven's movies."

"Holy crap," said Robert. "Are there cameras in that area?"

"No, the cameras are up, but not wired yet. There are motion sensors, but the results are going to show Jennifer moving and can be rebuked because of that."

"We should not continue the investigation. That is the scariest thing I have ever encountered and I no longer feel this investigation will be safe. Someone is going to get hurt or killed. These are evil, nothing less. Just pure evil."

"We have to do this investigation. Our reputations is on the line, not to mention how much the network paid for us to be here and for all the new and extra equipment."

"Staying alive should be worth more than that," said Jennifer.

"Anyone who does not want to go in tonight, can stay outside and monitor the equipment. But we are going in. We may be able to find out if the things you think you saw had something to do with the disappearance of the teenagers and others," said Robert. "If you decide to stay outside, this will be your last night on the show. Film your farewell and it will air after this episode."

"So, it's either go in or get out?" asked Hunter.

"That is entirely up to you," said Robert. "Make your choice."

"Sounds like we really do not have a choice," said Hunter.

"No you don't. I know how much you all like the paychecks the network gives you after every investigation," said Robert. "I expect every one of you to be ready to go as soon as the sun sets. Grab your equipment and meet me in front of the house."

Robert headed to the van. They made their choice, though each was scared. Walking away slowly, they went to get what they needed for the investigation.

"Let's get this done," said Robert.

Jennifer signaled McKenna and they walked away from the group.

"Should we even be in the house now?" asked McKenna.

"No. Upstairs I couldn't breathe they were so close to me, it was suffocating. I could feel their hands on me, pushing and grabbing me. It was the first time I had ever felt that," said Jennifer rubbing her arms where she had felt the hands. She remembered the cold of the fingers that grabbed her arms. "The ones downstairs confirmed to me that we need to get the heck out of here. Something bad is going to happen and it won't if we do not continue. Someone, maybe all of us, are going to die. This house needs to be burned to the ground. Whatever is in there is ancient and evil. Demons of some sort, I think, or just very ancient, evil. That was the most scared I have ever been."

"Robert is not going to stop this investigation. There is too much money riding on this episode," McKenna said.

"There has to be something we can do," said Jennifer.

Together they headed to the van and pulled out the property records. They flipped through the files that Amanda got from the county records department. While Jennifer scanned through the paperwork, McKenna went to try and talk some sense into the rest of the crew. There were property records showing when Michaels bought the property. It read that the land was owned by the state and it was bought from the state. There were some stories from locals about Michaels and a local tribe saying the house was on tribal land, it was a burial place, and/or he killed some sacred tree that kept evil spirits at bay. But nothing else. On paper it seemed like an everyday old house, but she knew different. She had felt it.

"Find anything that can scare Robert into not going in?" asked McKenna. "His mind is made up and he is only seeing dollar signs."

"Sure, but it is all stories passed on neighbor to neighbor. Who knows what is true?" she asked. "And I remember how stubborn he is. Took how many investigations for him to accept that I am not faking?"

"What can we do? They are scared. But they won't budge," she said. "They are going in no matter how scared they are."

"We need to stall them. I need to check again and see if what I saw was real or just my mind playing tricks on me."

"Are you doubting what you saw?"

"A little. Something does not seem right," said Jennifer. "I want to check again. If I get the same feelings, I will convince them to stay out. Even if we have to lock them in the van with James. If I get nothing then I will go in with you guys."

"I will try to stall," said McKenna.

"Unplug some of the cameras. That will take at leave 10 minutes before James realizes they are just unplugged," suggested Jennifer, grabbing a infrared camera and heading back to the house.

Jennifer walked around the house, hoping to feel something from the quiet voice again. Scanning with the camera. Nothing was showing up. She found a stone bench and sat down. Nothing.

She got up and headed to the porch. There was nothing there either. Like it was she imagined the whole thing. She pressed the mic.

"McKenna," she said. "Whatever was there earlier is gone. I am getting nothing now. Maybe it was my imagination. I am going to head back into the house and see what I get there."

"Got it," said McKenna. "Be careful."

"I will. I am going to stay in the doorway, so I can run out if anything happens."

She opened the door and stepped inside. The monitor showed nothing when she scanned it around the room and up the stairs. Suddenly there were invisible hands all over her, pulling and tugging at her. She managed to break free and fall out the door onto the porch.

The monitor showed several white figures in the doorway; they were invisible to her. She looked back at the monitor and tried to scoot away. She felt hands on her ankles as she was dragged back into the house. The door slammed with her still inside on the floor.

She needed to stop the team from doing the investigation. She tried to stand, but they were on her. They pushed her down and held her there. She tried to scream but the overpowering feeling of being squished made it impossible for her to get the oxygen needed to breathe let alone scream. She was suffocating. Her legs lifted and they started to drag her further into the house.

She managed to get enough breath to let out a blood curdling scream, shocking them in to temporarily letting her go. She scrambled to her feet and managed to get the door open before it was slammed shut again. Her breath left her body as she felt them on her again. They dragged her into the basement where they let her go and when she looked in the monitor, they were gone. She was alone. She screamed as loud as she could and hoped the others would hear her.

It was dark in the basement. Feeling around in the dark, there was nothing but dirt and rocks. She crawled slowly, feeling for the stairs, running into dirt walls and wooden posts, but no stairs. Her name was being called out. The team was all in the house looking for her. She tried yelling.

No matter how much she yelled, they still could not hear her. She could hear them, but they could not hear her. She felt like she was in a glass box with one way glass. She could hear and see them but to them she was silent and invisible. How was she going to get their attention? She needed to get them out of the house before someone was killed. She could hear the creatures shuffling all around her, but she could not see them. They were waiting.

Chapter 5

The investigators exited the house after searching it for the last 30 minutes for Jennifer. She was not in the house that they could tell. They did a thorough search, but there was nothing. Not even the creatures she had claimed to see.

Robert started giving instructions for the investigation; trying to rush through. They had spent too much of the evening looking for Jennifer. He feared the thirty minutes that they lost would impact their investigation negatively. They could have missed an important EVP or some other video evidence. He could see the excitement and fear of everyone in the group.

Worrying why and how she had disappeared; he put on a good front. They needed to get inside and get something that will make the network happy. A happy network meant more money for them.

"We will go inside in groups of two, room by room," he started. "EVPs will be done in every room for at least 15 minutes. James, you go over all the cameras and EVPs as soon as they are in your possession. We need to be able to give this town some answers."

"What about Jennifer?" asked McKenna. "She said she was going back inside and we all heard her scream."

"Maybe she is trying to scare us off so she can get her own show. Who knows," said Robert.

"Her own show?" asked Yoh.

"I overheard her on the phone at the hotel, talking to someone about the name of her show," explained Robert. "Something about the teenaged boys and more money."

"She never wanted that," said Amanda. "We talked about that before. She just wants to help people. This has never been about money for her."

"But the right amount can change anyone's mind," said Hunter. "Let's get in there. I am anxious to see what we get tonight."

"OK. Hunter and Yoh will be our first group in, Donovan and McKenna second, Ryan and Darlene third and finally Jessica and myself. Concentrate on the room that we know Yoh got a reading in earlier. Then we can work our way around the house."

James headed to the van as Robert continued giving his normal before-the-investigation speech. He never went inside the houses that they investigated. His job was to make sure the equipment was working and alerting the crews inside the house where there was any activity. Most of the time, the houses they investigated were duds and they got nothing, so he had been fabricating evidence. Robert and the network were in on it. Ratings were everything to them. It never mattered that they could scare occupants of some of the houses they investigated. It was all about the ratings. Bigger ratings meant they could get better companies for commercials.

Tonight he doubted fabricating evidence would be necessary. This house gave him a creepy feeling from the first time he walked in. His vantage point made it seem like the house was staring at him. Even while he was wiring the cameras and other equipment, he had felt like something was looking over his shoulder the entire time.

As he was running back the camera at the top of the stairs, a flash of something caught his eye. He ran it back again and there it was. A face in the camera; skinny, gray face with black, stringy, matted hair stared back at him. Its black holes for eyes, drew James in and he could not stop looking. Its black hole for a mouth opened and black goo came out. The face looked like it was screaming, but the camera's audio was not working. He rewound it again to see if he could see where the face came from, but it was there and then it wasn't.

He picked up his headset and asked Robert to come to the van. When Robert got there, he was accompanied with his partner for the night. Rewinding the tape, James told them to watch and tell him what they saw.

"What the hell was that?" Jessica asked.

"You saw that right? It was not just me?" asked James.

"Yes. It looks like Jennifer described. Like it climbed out of the pit of hell," said Robert. "She wasn't making anything up. Holy crap. Make a copy of that and add it to the hard drive for the Network so that can be shown at the end of the show."

"Already done."

"Great. Let's not tell the rest. I don't want them to start seeing that thing everywhere," said Robert. "We need to keep this investigation unbiased. It's bad enough Jennifer told them, but I think they think it was her making it up."

"We are still going in?" asked Jessica. "Did you even see what was on the camera? Or do you not even care?"

"Proof of evil creatures could make us rich, not to mention the network will give us whatever we want. I think it's worth it," he explained. "Besides they did not hurt Jennifer, they just scared her."

"I don't want to go in," said Jessica. "I will stay out here with James and monitor the video screens. I am scared, truly scared for the first time since I started doing this."

"No, you will go in or you can quit and I will make sure you never work on any show ever again."

"What?" she said. "Are you threatening me?"

"Make your choice. You have until the first two go in. After that you can head back to the hotel with Amanda and then I never want to see you again."

Robert turned and walked away. Amanda was warning them to be careful because the house should have been demolished years ago, so it was not very safe. She also did not participate with the investigations. She did the research and then stayed in contact by phone from her hotel room. He hoped that Jessica would not be going with her. Jessica was a great investigator and he hated to lose her, but he needed the network to be happy. He wanted a better time slot them 11 pm on Sunday night.

"We are ready. Want us to start on the staircase?" asked Yoh. He and Hunter were hoping not to have an experience like Jennifer did earlier. They both had been on several investigations where nothing ever happened, but they did not want to meet any of those creatures she had told them about.

"Get in there and get this investigation started," said Robert, giving each a manly hug. He watched them walk into the house as Jessica appeared at his side.

"I knew you would not let me down," he smiled.

"I am only going in to hopefully help the parents get closure. That is all. Not for you. For them," she said and walked away from him.

Hunter and Yoh turned on their body cameras once they crossed the threshold and headed through the house. Their flashlights shone on the missing floorboards and into the basement. They saw what was left of the kitchen and the rest of the rooms downstairs.

Robert had told them to check out the mirror and see if anything was there. They stood in front of it and tried to get some readings. As they were looking at the infrared monitor, Yoh caught something out of the corner of his eye. When he looked up, he caught a glimpse of a boy in the mirror. It disappeared as soon as he turned his head to get Hunter's attention.

"Did you get that on the monitor?" Yoh asked.

"There was a cold spot for about 10 seconds, but that was it," Hunter said. "It was there and then it was gone. What did you see? Mine looked like a shape."

"Like a boy, but it was so fast, I can't be sure."

They ran back the monitor and there it was. A ten second cold spot that had the shape of a body. Hunter relayed to Robert what they had and waited to see if he had anything to add.

"Robert says to go upstairs to the room that you got the EVP in," explained Hunter.

"Are you ready to check upstairs?" asked Yoh.

"Let's go. Maybe we will get more. Something longer than 10 seconds," said Hunter.

They walked slowly up the stairs. Yoh walked somewhat backwards up the stairs scanning most of the downstairs with the infrared camera. Hunter walked forward and hoped they got something.

"Wait," said Yoh stopping on the middle of the stairs. "What the hell is that?"

He pointed at 6 shapes on the infrared monitor, glowing white and an indication that they were cold. The shapes moved slowly up the stairs after them.

"Holy crap. Is it recording?"

"You better believe it," said Yoh. "James, is the camera on the stairs working?"

"Yes," James answered. "Are you seeing something?"

"We got 6 cold spots on the monitor coming up the stairs. Looks like they have human shapes."

"I am checking the recording as we talk and there is nothing there," said James. "Is your equipment recording?"

"Yes, we have recorded everything since we came inside," said Hunter.

"We need to make sure it is not a glitch. Span away from the spots and scan Hunter for 30 seconds and then go back."

"Got it," said Yoh.

He scanned Hunter just as James requested. When he turned the camera back to where the spots were seen, they were still there; closer this time.

"They are still there and now they are closer," said Yoh.

"What do you want us to do?" asked Yoh.

"Head upstairs and do an EVP session. See what they want," requested Robert.

Hunter and Yoh finished climbing to the top of the stairs. They stopped and did a quick EVP session.

"Who are you?"

"What do you want?"

"Where you the ones that scared Jennifer earlier?"

They waited a few seconds between each question. The infrared monitor turned off at the mention of Jennifer. When they turned it back on, the 6 cold spots were gone. There was a rush of cold that went past them that took their breath away quickly.

The door to their right opened and Hunter and Yoh could hear tapping coming from that room. Making sure all of their equipment was working, they headed slowly to the room. Yoh scanned the room first with the infrared camera before entering. Hunter followed all while keeping his back to Yoh's.

Inside the room, there was nothing but the chair that had been there earlier that day. They looked around the room. The tapping was all around them but there was no source of the sound. They were the only two in the room. The curtains blew in the breeze that was coming from the open window. The closet door was open, but there was nothing in there either.

Scanning the room, they did a quick EVP and then started to leave the room. The tapping sound started again. This time it was coming from right above their heads. Cautiously they looked up and scanned the ceiling with their flashlights. Crouching on the ceiling was a gray skin covered skeleton with black hair. Its hair hugged its head like it was not on the ceiling. It looked down at them, with its black holes for eyes. They retreated further into the room.

The creature scooted across the ceiling like a four legged spider, staying close to just above their head. They moved around trying to get to the door, but the creature was always between them and the door. Suddenly the creature stood on the ceiling and was right in their faces. It grabbed Yoh by the head and lifted him up to the ceiling. Both Hunter and Yoh screamed in terror.

"What is going on?" James yelled. Everyone could hear them screaming in the microphones and outside the house.

"Hunter! Yoh!" yelled Robert. "Talk to us!"

Hunter grabbed Yoh by the legs and tried to pull him out of the creature's grasp. It was too strong. Yoh was kicking and screaming, making it hard for Hunter to keep hold of his legs. Yoh used his hands to try to break the creatures grip on his head. The creature pulled Yoh closer to his face and bit the nose off. Blood poured out and down his face. Yoh screamed louder and Hunter pulled harder. Finally they heard the rest of the crew yelling as they ran up the stairs to try and help them.

They all rushed into the room, not even bothering to look up. Robert grabbed one of Yoh's legs and Donavon grabbed another.

The rest grabbed onto Hunter and took him out of the room. They watched as the creature pulled Yoh up closer and bit a large chunk of flesh out of his neck. Blood squirted all over the room and the remaining crew. Yoh stopped struggling. They let go of his legs and backed away, finally looking at what had a hold of Yoh. Robert recognized it from the video.

The investigation crew headed down the stairs, just as the front door slammed shut. Hands grabbed at them and tried to drag them back upstairs. Icy fingers that were invisible and hard to shake. They managed to get downstairs, but the door would not open.

"James, get the door open!" screamed Robert into the mic.

They looked out the side window and saw James running towards them with a crowbar. He put the crowbar between the door and the door jam, but it would not budge. He tried breaking the door with it, but it was like the door was impenetrable.

"We are going to try the back door," yelled Robert.

"Try a window. Break the glass," suggested James, remembering that the floor by the backdoor was in the kitchen and the floor there was too dangerous to walk on for one person let alone all of them.

They rushed into the living room to try to go out one of the already broken windows, but the feeling of suffocation was too overpowering. They again backed out of the room and headed toward the study. The feeling of suffocation was gone once they stepped into the room. Grabbing a metal poker by the fireplace, Donovan tried breaking the windows. Nothing. The poker just bounced off like they were made of rubber.

"I've got white on the monitor coming towards the room," said Ryan.

Donovan dropped the poker and closed the door to the study. He backed away, into the center of the room with the rest of the team. Tapping could be heard on the door and on the walls, but the monitor showed nothing in the room with them. They scanned the room with their flashlights, especially the ceiling. Nothing had come into the room with them.

"What the hell is going on?" said Darlene. "What was that?"

"Ghosts are not supposed to be able to hurt you," said McKenna. "How is this happening?"

"I told you," said Jessica pointing a finger at Robert. "You should have shown them the video. If you did, Yoh would still be alive and we would all be in our hotel rooms."

"What video?" asked Hunter.

"There is a video of one of those creatures that Robert and I saw right before Hunter and Yoh went in," explained Jessica. "Robert was more worried about making the network upset, then he was about our safety. He only sees in dollar signs. Jennifer warned us. He saw proof on the video and said nothing."

"How come you never said anything then?" said Darlene. "You could have."

"He threatened to fire me. But yes I should have, I will admit that. I screwed up," said Jessica.

"Who cares who is to blame right now? We need to get out of here before the rest of us get killed," said Hunter. He had Yoh's blood all over him.

"They are not coming in here, so maybe we are safe in here?" asked Darlene.

"No. We can't stay in here. Whatever is out there, I am not sure why they haven't come in here yet. They could just be trying to make us feel secure. They will get in here, we just do not know when," said Ryan.

"What can I do?" asked James via the mic. "There is no cell service out here and Amanda won't be back until tomorrow morning."

"My keys are in the cup holder of my truck," said Ryan. "Get into town and bring back anyone who has a gun or can get the door open."

"I will be back as soon as I can," promised James. He ran to the truck, found the keys and headed into town. The faster he got help, the better chance of them surviving this.

Chapter 6

They watched his tail lights disappear as the truck turned down the dirt driveway on his way to get help. Tapping on the walls and door continued, getting louder as more seemed to join the pack. Plaster dust fell from the walls as the walls vibrated it off. The creatures would make it through the walls before James got back. Something needed to be done.

"Any ideas?" asked Donovan. "We can't stay in here much longer. They're gonna get through the wall soon."

"If that happens James won't make it back with help, only to identify the bodies, if they leave any," said Robert.

"Not sure what the glass on the windows in this house are made of, but how do we get out of here? Can we go through the other wall?" asked Ryan.

"If they can, then we should be able to also," said Donovan.

He shone his light around until he saw a small hole in the wall next to the fireplace.

"What's on the other side of that wall?" asked Donovan, pointing at the hole.

"When we were mapping out the house for the equipment, I think there was a bathroom or mudroom right there. There was a door that looked like it went to the outdoors," said Hunter. "But this place is so big, I can't tell you for sure."

"What if the creatures are in there?" asked Jessica. "We have no idea what's on the other side of there. They could be waiting for us."

"Look," said Robert. "The plaster is not falling off there. They seem to be focusing on the wall by the door. Plus I don't hear any tapping on that way either."

Robert and Ryan both double checked the wall before Donovan started hitting it with the poker. The plaster broke off in chunks with every hit. He stopped every few hits to be sure that they hadn't moved. Soon there was a good amount of lathing showing. Ryan and Robert started pulling at the wood, trying to expose the lath on the wall on the other side, all while checking for the creatures on the other side.

"Shh!" said Darlene. "The tapping stopped."

"Crap," said Robert. "Stop."

"Maybe they got bored," said Ryan, continuing to break through the wall in the other room. "We need to keep going."

"No, we need to stop," said Darlene. "Why would they give up? After what it did to Yoh, I don't think it's gonna be that easy."

"You stop then," said Ryan. "Need the hole big enough to look through."

When his hole was about the size of a beach ball, he stuck his head through the hole.

"I said stop," said Robert, pulling him out. "What're you doing?"

"Trying to see if there is a door," he said. "No point of breaking through if there's nothing there."

He stuck his head back through, looking through the dark.

"We need to make it a little bigger," he said removing his head. "I need to be able to get my arm in with a flashlight. It's too dark to see anything."

Donovan handed him the poker. He was tired and did not want to do anymore. "Sorry," said Donovan. "I need a minute. You're gonna have to make the hole bigger yourself."

"No prob," Ryan said.

Ryan hit at the wall a few more times until he could make the hole bigger. The tapping started up again. They all looked at each other as he handed the poker back to Donovan and grabbed a flashlight.

"Give me a boost," said Ryan.

Robert and Donovan each grabbed a leg and helped him to get his arm with the flashlight through before his head. Once through he switched on the flashlight and shone it around. The door was there. He pulled his head out, leaving his arm in the hole.

"Hunter was right," he said. "There's a door, but I am not sure if it goes outside. It's really dark to see too much even with the flashlight."

"If I remember, it was a storm door of some sort," said Hunter. "Really strong and thick."

"OK. We need to get this hole bigger so we can all fit through and get out of this place," said Ryan.

Suddenly he felt cold, bony fingers grab his wrist and yank hard. Ryan slammed against the wall. Chunks of plaster fell off the wall and the broken lathing cracked under the strength of the creature pulling on his arm. He placed his other hand against the wall and pushed.

He screamed as he tried to pull his arm free.

Donovan, Robert and Hunter grabbed his body and pulled. Ryan felt more fingers grabbing his arm and pulling. He screamed as one of the creatures bit into his arm. The pain was excruciating. It felt like his arm was being ripped off.

"Pull harder," yelled Donovan.

Together the three of them were able to break him loose from their grasp. He continued to scream holding his arm. Blood was pouring from his hand and arm. Robert and Hunter held him still while Donovan tried to pull his hand away to see how bad it was.

Ryan's hand was gone and so was most of the bone and flesh in his forearm. From his elbow down was only skin and some flesh. He let go to keep himself from vomiting. Gathering his composure he went back to Ryan.

"Darlene, bring me your first aid kit," he yelled. "I need a belt or rope or something to make a tourniquet. They severed his artery. He's gonna bleed out if we don't stop it. Do you have anything?"

"I have this," said McKenna, pulling the bandanna out of her hair. "Can this work?"

"I will make it," he said. "Just tie it above his elbow."

"What?" she asked. "What the..?"

She covered her mouth and tried not to vomit. She was trained in first aid, but not for anything this horrific. She tied the bandanna as tight as she could and moved away from him quickly. He screamed when Donovan poured alcohol on what was left of his forearm. Donovan tied the bandanna tighter. The bleeding slowed but did not stop. Ryan had lost too much, there was nothing else they could do for him.

He pushed back onto his knees.

Darlene wiped the blood off the best she could and then pulled herself back together quickly and moved back towards him. She rested against the wall to catch her breath and again tried not to vomit.

"Darlene!" yelled McKenna, running towards her.

Darlene stood up as hands reached through the hole and grabbed her by the shoulders. The creatures were strong and fast. By the time they got to her, she was halfway through the wall. They were all around her, grabbing and pulling at her. She felt herself being pulled back into the room. Trying to help she placed her hands on the hole above her and tried to push herself out of their grasp.

Pieces of wood ripped through her shirt and into her skin as she was forced through the hole again. The smell of the blood from her scratches and from Ryan's body fueled them on. They savagely fought to pull their victim in with them. She landed hard on some of the creatures and tried to scramble to her feet.

Fighting them off was pointless as she was quickly overpowered and fell to the floor. Kicking and screaming, she tried her hardest to stay alive. Pain ripped through her legs as creatures bit and ripped at her skin. Her arms were ripped from their sockets and creatures fought over them. She screamed one last time until everything didn't hurt anymore. .

They could hear her screaming as the creature tore her apart. Others ripped at the edges of the hole, making it bigger so they could get in. Darlene's screaming stopped suddenly. She was gone.

The creatures reached towards them wanting to take them too. Their hands and arms covered in blood. There was no time to mourn their friends. They needed to get out of that room as fast as possible. The creatures would be through the wall soon and they needed to get out of there. Only the door they came in was a possible exit.

"What do we do?" yelled Jessica. "They're getting in."

"We can try the door and see if we can make it out," said Robert.

"They are breaking though. Go! Go for the door," said Robert. He grabbed McKenna's arm and dragged her to the door. Donovan pushed Jessica towards the door. She had been frozen in terror against the wall, eyes wide in fear.

"I am gonna open the door and start swinging," he said. "When I do, run."

"Where?" asked Jessica.

"Upstairs, I don't care as long as it's away from them."

He placed his hand on the door knob and turned. Jennifer was on the other side of the door.

"Follow me," she said as she grabbed Jessica's hand and ran up the stairs quickly but carefully.

The creatures starting pouring out of the room where they had dragged in Darlene and the room the team was just in. The team all scrambled up the stairs, creatures hands reaching for them. They followed Jennifer.

She ran past the room where Yoh was killed. Robert paused and looked inside the room. Yoh's body was not there but blood and pieces of flesh were all over the room. Looking down he saw bloody footprints going downstairs.

Jennifer had led them to a room at the end of the hall that overlooked the east side of the house. It was a large room with a metal bed frame and remnants of a desk or dresser in it. The door was stronger and had a lock on it. Though the creatures did not seem to be able to open a door, they still locked it.

"What the hell is going on?" asked Jennifer. "I saw Ryan on the floor. I'm gonna guess by all the blood that whatever those are killed him?"

"Yes," said Robert. "They pulled Darlene through the wall and they killed Yoh earlier tonight."

"I could hear the screaming," she said. "Where's James?"

"He took Ryan's truck into town to get help," said Donovan. "He left about an hour ago. Hopefully he will be back with help soon. What happened to you?"

"Long story for when we get out of here, but we won't last that long at this rate," said Jennifer facing Robert and pointing at him. "I told you not to come in here! Why? You saw the creature on the recording. Their deaths are your fault. 100% your fault."

"Wait!" said Donovan. "You saw one of the creatures on video and still let us come in here? You could have stopped this. What is wrong with you?"

"Wrong with me?" he asked. "I thought the risk was minimal. She said they couldn't hurt us."

"I said *spirits* cannot hurt you," said Jennifer. "I don't do things like this. This is all new to me."

"I took you at your word," said Robert.

"My word?" she said. "I told you not to come in here. What about that word?"

"I heard you tell McKenna that you thought it was the spirits messing with you," he said. "Even you doubted your abilities."

"Stop!" said McKenna. "Fighting is not gonna get us out of here. We have to work together or we're gonna die."

"Yes," said Donovan. "Can we break the windows?"

Hunter picked up a branch that had fallen through a hole in the roof and hit the window. The branch bounced off, just like the other windows downstairs. He threw it down in disgust.

"Nothing," said Hunter. "What about the hole in the roof? Can we get out that way?"

"Maybe, but we need to be careful," said Robert. "We don't know if they are in there or where they might be."

"We have to try something," said Jessica. "I don't want to wait here for them to kill us too."

"Wait," said Donovan. "We need to think about this. I'm not interested in becoming their next meal. Plus we don't know where they are right now."

"Probably finishing up Darlene and Ryan," said Hunter sarcastically.

"I say we try the roof," said Jennifer. "It's the only way. They could be here any second."

"OK," agreed Donovan. "But we need to be very careful. I don't want to give them any way to know what we are doing. Is that desk strong enough for one of us to stand on it?"

Hunter and Robert carefully moved the desk to just under the hole in the roof. Donovan climbed up and carefully peaked his head through with a light. He shone the light around looking for the creatures. They weren't there, but something else was.

Donovan dropped down. He sat down on the desk and put his hands on his head.

"Are they up there?" asked Robert.

"No," said Donovan. "But I know where the boys disappeared to. Or what is left of them."

Chapter 7

"What do you mean?" asked McKenna. "They searched the entire house. There was nothing up there."

"There's something up there now," said Donovan.

Robert took the flashlight from Donovan and climbed up to see it for himself. He spanned the light around until he saw it. There was a pile of half-eaten bodies in the corner. From everything that they read about the missing boys, what remained of their clothes matched. He heard a sound behind him and he swung around fast.

Squatting in the corner was a shape, huddled up tight. This was not one of the creatures, he was sure of that. He shined the light at its head. It turned its head towards him lightning fast. It was Yoh. He had black eyes like the creatures with the same black goo coming from his mouth and ears. The bite marks from the creatures oozed it also. Yoh seemed to be holding something in his hands. He slowly put down what was in his hands and got into a crouched position facing Robert. Robert gasped when he saw Darlene's watch on what Yoh put down. His gasp caused Yoh to charge at him. Yoh was almost to him when Robert dropped out of the hole.

"What?" asked Donovan.

"It was Yoh," said Robert. "But it was one of those creature versions of Yoh. He was chewing on Darlene's arm."

Jessica whimpered and squatted down by the window. McKenna kneeled down next to her, trying to comfort her. This was turning out to be the worst investigation ever. Demons exist and can hurt you. This was not what she had signed up for.

"We have to get out of here," she said.

"How?" asked Robert. "We're trapped."

"Not sure what you saw, but there is nothing up there now," said Hunter coming down from looking in the hole. "No Yoh, and no pile of bodies. I think these things are playing with our heads. The hole is big enough for us to get through, we just need to hurry."

"I saw the bodies," said Donovan. "What's going on here?"

"Where's Sam and Dean when you need them?" said McKenna.

"What the..?" said Robert. "How are fictional characters from a television show gonna help us?"

"After what we've seen," she said. "I'm willing to take that risk. They always got their shit together and make it out alive. We'd have a better chance of survival with them at this point."

"Whatever," said Robert. "Donovan, you go first and then you can pull the girls up."

"Got it," Donovan said.

He carefully climbed back into the ceiling hole. Spanning the light around, he saw nothing. He pulled himself up and balanced on two wooden beams. The hole in the roof was large enough, but the beams and shingles around it looked very unstable. He pulled himself out and found a safe place to stand to pull the rest of them out.

"Ok," said Donovan. "Send 'em up."

"Jessica," said Robert gesturing for her to come to him.

She climbed up on the desk with him and he helped her get to Donovan's hands. Donovan pulled her out and helped her to get to a sturdy section of the roof. McKenna was next then Jennifer, then Hunter and finally Robert pulled himself through. Once they were all out on the roof, they looked to see which would the safest way off.

"It looks like if we climbed that way," said Donovan shined his light to the left of where they were. "We can get to the porch and jump off."

"The roof is worse there, though," said Robert. "Any other options?"

"Any other way and we have to jump about 25 feet and more than likely break our legs in the fall," said Donovan. "This way we climb down to the porch and jump a shorter distance. Less likely we break our legs."

"OK," said Robert. "Somebody needs to test the roof and find a safe path across. No point in going that way if the roof won't hold us."

"I'll do it," volunteered Hunter. "I'm the heaviest. If it can hold me, then the rest of you will be easy."

"Be careful," said McKenna. "We don't want to fall through or off."

Hunter carefully made his way across the roof, shining his light and testing the beams as he went. There were spots that looked safe, but after testing them they were not. Beams were stronger, but balancing was not going to be easy. After several attempts he finally managed to find a path that would hold them all, but only one at a time. There wasn't a lot of balancing, but it still would be tricky.

"We need to go one at a time," he explained coming back to where they waited on the roof. "Follow me and watch your feet. Use your flashlights."

"McKenna," said Donovan. "You go first and then I will follow with Jessica right behind me, Jennifer next and Robert behind her."

"Balancing was never my thing," said McKenna. "Pray I don't fall."

"There's not a lot of balancing, you just need to put your feet exactly where I put mine," said Hunter taking her hand and showing her the way.

The holes in the roof were near impossible to see with the moon behind the clouds. Flashlights helped a little but not too much. The way was slow, but soon they all managed to be at the edge just above the porch, Hunter laid on his stomach and shined his light to check for holes or apparent weak spots on the porch.

"It looks like going a few more feet this way, we can get down without any problem," said Hunter shining his light to the right.

The porch looked sturdy, but part of where they needed to get to looked like it was ready to crumble. The shingles, sheeting and beams were all missing. They would have to use part of the exposed outside wall to make it onto the roof of the porch. The only sturdy spot on the porch was by there.

"It's not gonna be easy, but we can do it," said Hunter. "At least I think-hope-we can."

Hunter lifted himself off his stomach onto his knees.

"Are you guys ready to try this?" he asked.

"Unless one of you can fly, I think this is our best bet," said Jennifer.

"I'm in," said Jessica. "If I fall, it's only 10 feet or so. Worse could be a broken ankle. Better than those things' meal."

"Let's hurry before I change my mind and remember that I'm terrified of heights," said McKenna.

They stood up and carefully started to inch towards where Hunter said to go. Hunter fell forward as hands reached through a hole in the roof and grabbed at his legs. He wrapped his arms around a beam trying to keep them from dragging him down. Donovan ran to help him, going around the hole they were grabbing at Hunter through. He stepped on a section that he thought was safe and heard a loud crack.

He felt himself falling. Trying to grab anything to keep from falling all the way through, but nothing was strong enough. Everything broke as he grabbed it. He waited for whatever was below him to break his fall. The staircase broke his fall. Wind knocked out of him, he moved limbs to be sure nothing was broken.

Pushing himself into a sitting condition, he felt the staircase shift. Before he could make it to a standing position he found himself falling again. The stairs pulled away from the wall and the second story landing. Wind knocked out of him again, he pushed himself into a sitting position. He felt a board shift under him. Slowly he turned around. The creatures jumped on him. He felt the pain as they ripped and tore at him. Blood filled his mouth as he coughed and choked from the blood filling his lungs.

Robert and McKenna fought hard to pull Hunter back onto the roof, but the creatures were too strong. They lost their grip on him as the creatures dragged him back inside. When Hunter opened his eyes, he watched from the ceiling as Donovan was torn apart by the creatures. The pieces of Donovan ripped from his body were dragged toward the kitchen. The creatures held Hunter on the ceiling as they started to tear at his body. They let go of him and he fell from the ceiling to the floor. He was already in so much pain that he didn't notice the fall broke some of his ribs.

He felt himself being dragged into the kitchen also. They creatures dragged him down on top of Donovan's dead body. The creatures ripped off his legs and scurried away from him. He was choking on his own blood. He gurgled as he tried to scream when one of the creatures ripped open his chest and yanked his heart from his chest.

Jessica and Jennifer stood in horror as they watched Hunter being dragged back down and Donovan falling through the roof. Two more of their friends were gone. They still needed to get down.

"Robert," said Jennifer. "We need to get off this roof. Now."

"OK," he said quietly. "We need to get back to that room."

"What about climbing down to the porch?" asked Jessica. "Why the room?"

"Did you just miss Donovan falling through and Hunter being yanked back into the house?" Robert asked. "We need to get back to where we know they can't get in and wait for James to get back here."

"Who knows how long that will be?" said Jennifer. "I'm getting off this roof. Jessica, McKenna, are you coming with me?"

"No," she said. "I can't do this anymore. I'm going back to the room with Robert."

"McKenna?"

"I'm with Robert," she said. "If you get down, wait for James and show them where we are."

"Are you sure?" Jennifer asked. "They might be in the room waiting for you."

"I will go in first and check," said Robert. "If it's clear, then they can climb down. If not, I'm dead and they can follow you off the roof."

Robert moved back towards the hole they had climbed through with McKenna and Jessica right behind him. He made it back to the hole and into the room without any problems. So did McKenna. After seeing they all made it down, Jessica started to lower herself back through. As she was halfway through, bony hands grabbed her and pulled her into the crawl space. Screaming, she curled into a ball and waited for them to kill her. Nothing happened. She opened her eyes to see them all staring over her, black goo dripping onto her body. She sat up as they all backed off slowly and disappeared into the walls.

She crawled over to the hole and down into the room. Robert and McKenna were shocked to see her.

"What happened?" asked McKenna.

"We saw them grab you!" said Robert.

"They just walked away and left me," said Jessica.

"What the hell is going on here?" said Robert. "They kill everyone else they take, but they leave you alive."

There was a loud thud behind them. Spinning around they saw it was Jennifer.

"Thought you were getting out of here?" asked McKenna.

"I heard Jessica scream," she said. "Came to see if maybe I could help. Maybe psychic?"

"Can you?" Robert asked.

"No," she said. "I can't feel them like I did the first time. Not sure why."

There was a scrapping sound behind them. McKenna screamed as she shined her light towards the noise. Creatures were climbing through and crawling across the ceiling. Robert ran to the door and opened it up. They ran through the hallway and stopped at the staircase. They had forgotten it was gone. Creatures jumped at them from the first floor using the fallen stairs to get them closer. They started pulling themselves up still reaching for them.

The creatures were now coming down the hall; crawling across the ceiling, walls and floor. They ran to the room they saw Yoh killed in and slammed the door shut. Robert took the chair that one of the team members had left in there and jammed it under the door knob. It wiggled but didn't open.

"What do we do now?" said McKenna. "We need to get out of here."

"Give me a second," yelled Robert. "I need to think."

"We wouldn't be in this mess if you had taken the time to think when you saw the video," said Jennifer.

Robert rushed at her and shoved her against the wall. A hand on each of her arms, he squeezed hard.

"Shut up," he yelled. "I screwed up. Stop reminding me."

"Let go of me," said Jennifer.

When he did not let go if her immediately, she brought her knee up and connected. His eyes grew wide and a funny scream came out of him. Sounded like what she kneed was now in his throat. He let go of her, grabbed himself and fell to the ground. She walked around him back to the others. Jessica and McKenna looked from her to Robert with their mouths open.

"How do we get out of here now?" asked Jessica moving away from Jennifer.

"We go out the door," she said. "That's all we can do. No other choice."

"How?" said McKenna. "They're outside. We're not getting through them and living to tell about it. We're as good as dead the minute we open that door."

"Maybe we can toss them Robert and make a run for it?" suggested Jennifer.

"So, we would sacrifice him to save ourselves?" questioned McKenna. "No way. He may be a complete jerk but feeding him to those things, I couldn't do it."

"He sacrificed all of you for ratings," said Jessica. "How's that fair? I say we let Karma get him. If he lives, he lives. If we live, we live. Better us then him."

"I won't help you kill him, but if you make it out," said McKenna. "Then I'll follow."

"We need to go then," said Jennifer. She removed the chair and grabbed the door. "Stand behind me. Maybe we can get out while they are running at him."

"Ok," said Jessica. She grabbed McKenna and dragged her behind Jennifer.

"Here we go," said Jennifer, opening the door.

Chapter 8

The creatures poured into the room and ran at Robert. He was still holding himself on the floor in a fetal position. Hiding behind the door, Jennifer, Jessica and McKenna went unseen by the creatures. After it looked like the last creature came into the room, Jennifer led them silently out of the room. Floorboards creaked once they were outside the room and in the hallway. Some of the creatures turned towards the sound, made an eerie sound and tried to charge after them. McKenna reached back to grab the door to yank it closed.

Creatures slammed into the closed door and made that sound again. It sent shivers down their backs. Jennifer shone the light around and looked for more of the creatures. So far there were none. The creatures would get out of that room and no one wanted to be in the house when they did.

The staircase was no help. Getting out that way was not going to happen. Jessica saw a door and ran for it. She swung it open and shone her light around.

"It's empty," she said turning towards Jennifer and McKenna. "We can hide here for now."

The room was suddenly filled with creatures. They grabbed Jessica and slammed the door shut. She managed to break free and made it to a window that was missing glass. Unsure as to why they just stood there watching her, not making any move to attack her. Taking in their hesitation as an advantage in her favor, she stuck one leg out the window. She was going to jump. Broken legs were better then being eaten alive. She swung her other leg out the window and twisted until she was on her stomach. Dangling from the window sill, she readied herself for the fall. When she let got, she landed on the ground just outside the back of the house.

Standing slowly, she tested to be sure nothing as broken. She kept a hand on the side of the house as she used her light to make her way back to the front of the house. As she made her way to the front of the house, she could hear scratching coming from above her. Stopping she looked up at the house. Creatures were crawling down the outside walls of the house, coming straight at her. She stood frozen in fear.

Before she could move, they grabbed her by the head and yanked her up the wall. She screamed and tried to break their hands free. Their fingers pressed harder and harder into her head. She felt a sharp pain as her skull cracked. They pulled her back into the house through the large hole in the wall by the roof.

Dragging her across the ceiling, the creatures threw her to the floor. She landed on part of the broken banister, piercing her back through to her chest. She looked at where it came through and cried. At least she would be dead before they could start eating her. Creatures swarmed her and started tearing at her body. Unfortunately, she didn't die until after they had ripped her body apart. Arms, legs, ribs. She died in agony, choking on her own blood.

McKenna and Jennifer stared frozen in shock as they watched the horrific way Jessica died. Robert screamed from the room. Where Jessica's screams stopped, his did not. They must be playing with him, keeping him alive until they had their fun. McKenna screamed as one of the creatures ripped open the top of Jessica's skull and pulled out her brain. Another bit out her eyes, while the other shared her brain with the others.

"Don't look," said Jennifer. "We need to find a way out of here."

"Some of these old houses had another staircase that led to the kitchen," McKenna said. "It was for the servants, so guests would not see them taking things to people upstairs."

"Are you sure?" she asked. "I don't remember one. I checked out the whole house earlier."

"It could be in a closet or in a room above the kitchen," said McKenna.

"I think there is a closet over here," said Jennifer. She shone her light back towards the room Robert was screaming from. There was a small door. McKenna carefully opened it while Jennifer shined her light inside. There was a narrow staircase.

"Let's go," she said. "Be careful though. We can't be sure if the creatures are at the other end or if it is as damaged as the main one."

"Lead the way," said Jennifer. She followed behind McKenna as she carefully took step by step, making their way into the kitchen.

"Shh," said McKenna.

They stopped and listened. Sounds of feet scurrying above them sounded very close. Nervously, Jennifer shined her light above them. Nothing. Not behind them. Not in front of them.

"It must be echoing from the room," said McKenna.

She continued down the stairs, shining her light around in front of her, looking for the creatures. They were not on the stairs at all.

Maybe they didn't know about this one, she thought to herself. They could get out of here without seeing the creatures again. She moved faster but still was careful. She did not want to jinx herself.

At the bottom of the stairs was another door; she carefully opened it. Half expecting to see the creatures, she held her breath. They were not there. Before she stepped into the kitchen, she remembered that half of the floor was gone. She shined her light onto the floor and carefully made her way across. Jennifer was close behind her, stepping where she stepped.

They made it to the dining room on the other side of the kitchen without falling or seeing any of the creatures. The floor creaked and they waited to be attacked. Nothing came. They inched through the dining room, checking for another way out. Both windows were broken with partial glass still in them. They could remove the rest of the glass, but that could be noisy. The room had no door, so there would be no way to keep he creatures away if they did hear them.

Jennifer remembered that the back door to the kitchen was barely hanging on to the jamb. They could pull it off and make it outside away from the house before the creatures could get to them.

"McKenna," she whispered. "The back door in the kitchen. We might be able to get it down and get outside before they get to us."

"There is almost no floor right there," McKenna whispered back. "We could use the door to get across that section of floor, but there is nothing to stand on to get the door down."

"Crap," she said. "What about the counters? We could stand on those."

"We could, but we have to be careful," McKenna said. "They look like they will fall about if you breathe on them wrong."

They made their way back to the kitchen. McKenna made her way to the cabinets to the left of the door, while Jennifer made her way to cabinets at the right of the door. Coordinating together silently they grabbed the door.

"On three," whispered Jennifer. "1, 2, 3."

They both pulled at the door. It made a loud creaking noise as it started to break away from the jamb.

"Almost got it," said McKenna. "Pull a little harder your way."

Jennifer tugged the door her way, pulling the door from the jamb. It fell to the floor with a bang so loud there was no way the creatures didn't hear it. McKenna climbed down from the cabinets and onto the door. Jennifer followed.

The weight of both was too much and the beams underneath the door gave way. They felt themselves falling. Jennifer grabbed the cabinet before they had fallen too far. McKenna did the same.

Scurrying footsteps came from behind them and stopped. Looking behind her, McKenna saw nothing.

She felt something drip on her hand. Terrified, she looked up; she was face to face with one of the creatures. She screamed as the creature bit into her hand. Letting go she fell into the basement.

"McKenna," screamed Jennifer as another creature jumped onto her back. It reached up and tore her fingers off the cabinet causing her to fall also.

McKenna landed on her back while fighting to keep the creature from biting her again. Her hand throbbed as she placed her hand under its chin pushing its head up. The creature grabbed her free hand and pinned it down to the floor in the basement. She screamed and tried to use her legs to roll the creature under her instead. Succeeding she pinned the creature under her. There was a piece of the basement wall laying just within her reach. She grabbed it and smacked the creature on the side of the head. It didn't even stun it. Part of its skull was crushed in with black goo pouring out. The creature fought harder and returned her to her back. It seemed mad now and was snapping and gnashing at her, spitting black goo all over her face.

She managed to get a leg between her and it when Jennifer fell into the basement. She kicked it off her and across the basement. Scrambling to her feet she pulled the creature off Jennifer's back. There were some bite marks on Jennifer's back. She helped her up and together they looked for a way out. They had lost their flashlights in the fall, so McKenna crawled on her knees looking for one while Jennifer kept the creatures away with a broken wood beam that had fallen through the kitchen floor.

Feeling around in the dark, she felt an arm. She yanked her hand away in fear. It was cold and stiff. She moved her hand back and found a camp lantern that must have been from the missing teens or from another victim. Digging in her pocket, she found a packet of matches. For the first time tonight, she was happy at something Robert made her do. She struck the match and prayed there was still gas in it. There was a whooshing sound as the gas was ignited by the flame. She turned up the gas, making it brighter and shined it on what she touched.

"What the …?" she exclaimed jumping up. She swung the lantern back to where Jennifer was standing. Her head was down and surrounded by creatures. Slowly Jennifer and the creatures moved towards McKenna.

"How?" she stammered.

"I am fine," she said. "We are all fine."

The creatures attacked her, knocking her onto Jennifer's mutilated body. Jennifer was the first victim of the creatures that night and somehow managed to fool them into thinking she was alive. McKenna frantically looked for a way out of the basement. Then she realized where she was.

This was not a basement- it was the opening of some sort of cave where the creatures lived. There was no door to the basement, but they had just assumed that there was one in a house this old. McKenna found a small hole and crawled into it. Jennifer kept the creatures off her just long enough so that she could escape through the hole. McKenna realized too late that this was part of her plan. Standing up she saw more creatures staring at her. She dropped the lantern, breaking the glass and igniting the debris inside the small hole.

Chapter 9

Robert screamed in terror as the creatures stood over him, watching him. He prayed that they would make it quick and that he would not feel any pain. How things had been going for him lately, he doubted anyone would answer his prayer. Opening his eyes, he saw more creatures above him crouching on the ceiling looking down at him. Black goo from them dripped onto him.

He continued screaming as they tried to grab him. They would stop suddenly and then another few would try. As if they were playing with him, enjoying his screams. They stood close, but never touching him.

He managed to make his way into a corner by slowly scooting backwards on the floor. Standing up, the creatures remained just out of arms reach from him. As if they were waiting for the command to attack. Wherever he moved, they kept the same distance from him. He slowly moved around the room keeping his back to the wall.

When he got to the door, he grabbed the door knob from behind his back There was no way he was going to put his back to them. They might be keeping him at bay but turning his back could make them attack. He carefully got the door open and stepped out. They kept their distance, but when he shut the door on them they attacked the door from inside the room.

As he entered the hallway he noticed that the house was filling with smoke. Looking from where the stairs once were, he could see that the kitchen section of the house was in flames. He looked for a place to hide and try to escape. The door to the room Jessica had run to was open. He headed there. Entering the room, he slammed the door shut. He coughed as smoke poured into the room from under the door. Moving away from the door, he tried to adjust his eyes to the dark.

The moon must have peaked out from the cloud cover because he could make out shapes in the dim light it provided. There was another bed frame and possibly another dresser. Tattered curtains blew in the small breeze through the open windows. There were not holes in the walls or ceiling in this room, so the debris from outside must have come from the open windows or from animals bringing it in.

He went to the window and looked out. Jumping was not an option, so he needed to try to climb out onto the roof. There was a small ledge between the first and second floor from the wood trim that he might be able to use to get to the porch roof that wrapped around to the side of the house. It would be easier to use a rope and then climb down but scaling the side of the house seemed like his best option. If he survived this, he was going to add a rope to the investigation kit.

Swinging his legs out, he reached for someplace to hold onto. There was another piece of wood trim just above the windows. He tested the wood trim and found it to be sturdy. Now to figure out how to use it to make his way to the porch. There was only about 2 inches of trim for him to use to walk and hold on to. He needed to be quick but extremely careful. Falling at this point would not be helpful. More than likely breaking his legs, leaving him as easy pickings for the creatures to get.

Just as he was about to start moving, there was a banging on the door.

"Robert," yelled Jennifer. "Let me in"

He climbed back into the room and opened the door. Jennifer was there and looked like she had rolling around in dirt. Smoke had filled the rest of the house and fire was slowly climbing up the wall to the second floor.

"Where's McKenna?" he asked, shutting the door as she entered the room.

"We made it downstairs and they creatures attacked us," she explained. "I managed to get away, but they dragged her into the basement."

"The staircase fell down," he questioned. "How did you even get downstairs? And if you were, how come you didn't just go out the kitchen door?"

"The floor by the door is nonexistent," she said. "McKenna figured out there was a hidden staircase for the help to use to get to the kitchen. They grabbed her as soon as we made it into the kitchen."

"What about the fire? How did that get started?"

"There was a camping lantern that we managed to light," she explained. "I dropped it trying to get back upstairs."

"Crap. We need to move fast then. This old house will burn fast," he said. "I think I figured a way out of here. Have you ever rock climbed before?"

"No,' she said. "I'm not really into outdoor sports. But I'm a fast learner."

"Then get ready for a quick lesson," he said. "It's either that, we burn to death or the creatures get us."

After five minutes of trying to explain to her what they were going to be doing, he decided it was time to try it. He moved towards the window and looked out. There were creatures all over the outside. He closed the window, hoping to keep them out until they could think of something else.

"We can forget about that now," he said turning around. "They are outside now. Maybe we can get to the other side and go back out to the roof. Hopefully that part is not in flames yet."

"Yes," she said. "I know."

"How?" he asked. "You said you couldn't get a read on them."

"Oh, I can read them," she said smiling evilly. "I can actually even tell them what to do."

"What?" he said. "Is this a joke?"

Jennifer walked to the door and opened it. Creatures crawled into the room from the walls, floor and ceiling. Robert backed up to the wall. She walked to the window to let them come in that way too. The creatures stayed away from him and behind her.

"What're you doing?" he yelled backing up to the wall. "Why're you letting them in?"

He watched as she stepped aside and Yoh, Hunter, Donovan, Ryan, Darlene, and Jessica walked into the room. They moved like the creatures. Their hair matted and hanging in their face. Covered in blood with black goo coming from their eyes, ears and mouth. Behind them came the missing boys. They also looked like his team. Then he realized they were dead. All of them.

"What is wrong with you?" he yelled.

"I am fine," she said.

"We are all fine," they all said together.

He screamed as they moved closer to him. He crouched down against the wall only to have Hunter and Yoh grab him and throw him into the middle of the room like he weighed nothing. He tried to scramble to the door, but it was closed by Darlene. Members of his team took turns tossing him back into the middle of the room when he tried to get to the wall. Every time it was like they had super human strength.

They each drooled black goo down their blood-covered clothes and body. They moved like the creatures, slow at times but lightning fast when they wanted to. The parts of their bodies were in one piece but had black oozing from the bite marks. Their skin was grey covering bones with their clothes ripped and tattered.

He lay on his back in pain from being thrown around the room. He screamed as Yoh bit into his leg. Hunter and Ryan grabbed onto his arms and pulled at them until his shoulders dislocated. Jessica and Darlene tore at his chest, ripping through his stomach pulling out his intestines and internal organs. His arms ripped from his body. Screaming in pain, he looked up to see Jennifer standing over his head.

"We are all fine," she said as she ripped through his chest and yanked out his heart. "We are fine." She bite into it, chewing as blood poured out of her mouth.

Chapter 10

James drove behind the sheriffs' car and the fire trucks as they pulled in front of the Michael's house. It was engulfed in flames, smoke pouring from the windows. The fireman stood just outside the fence surrounding the house and watched it burn.

"What're you doing?" he yelled. "My friends are in there."

"There's no way anyone could still be alive in that," said the fire chief. "Besides, it's better that it burns. It can burn to nothing for all I care."

James watched in shock as not one of the rescue workers he brought back tried to help his friends or put out the fire. They all stood and watched as the roof of the house fell in. Soon the chimneys followed. Glass exploded in the heat. The front of the house fell in and soon the back did too. The porch was the last thing to fall. Even after everything fell, they did nothing but watch. It would take hours and they would wait. The house soon fell into the earth, into what they thought was the basement.

The flames grew higher and smoke poured out of the firepit the collapse of the house made. The fireman stood by with water from their water trucks just in case the fire spread to the trees and bushes that surrounded the house. The large tree caught but they put that out fast, all without stepping inside the fence. The sheriff called for an ambulance just in case, but the van from the morgue was already on site.

James remembered the video equipment was recording in the van still. He opened the back door and climbed in. Rewinding all the footage took a while. There was at least two hours' worth of recordings on each of the ten cameras. He scanned the footage and found nothing. Most of the cameras had malfunctioned and recorded nothing but static.

One camera, though. had footage of Donovan falling from what looked like the roof. He watched as the staircase with Donovan on it pulled away from the wall and crashed into the floor below it. Then static. There was no more video, no audio recordings. Nothing. Just static or fuzz. Even the original footage of the creature was gone. Erased.

There was nothing from inside the house, but there was something from inside the van. No one knew that he had a hidden camera in there. Crew members had accidentally erased or damaged his equipment before, so he had it installed. Playing back the video, he watched Jennifer open the back door and climb inside. She found the video of the creature and erased it. She also disconnected all his equipment.

"What the heck is going on?" he asked himself. He watched the video as Jennifer got up and left the van.

He climbed out of the van and headed back to where the rescue workers were watching the house continue to burn. The flames were smaller with the smoke getting darker. A smell of something burning and rotting was emanating from the hole. It smelled like a campfire that was cooking road kill. He gagged as did everyone else who smelled it.

"What is that smell?" asked one of the sheriff's deputies. "It smells like death."

Handkerchiefs came out and covered mouths and noses. Some fireman put on their oxygen to avoid the stench. Soon the wind blew the opposite way and gave them a reprieve from the gross smell. It grew worse the longer the house burned. Most stopped watching and headed back to their vehicles.

After another hour, the sheriff and all the firemen left. The house was gone, and no one cared to try to check for any embers. Soon it would be ash, but at least the house would be gone. The deputies who stayed waited until there was no more smoke before they called in a crew to help fill the hole with dirt.

It was late afternoon when a truck came loaded with dirt and another loaded with workers. James stuck around hoping that maybe one of them survived. Highly doubtful, but he hoped. The truck backed up by the hole and started to lift the back.

"It's not gonna be enough dirt, but at least it will put out some of the embers," said one of the deputies. "Better call in for another couple loads."

"They got here pretty fast," said James.

"Once the sheriff saw it was on fire," he explained. "He called in for it. Wanted any memory of this house and its history gone. Covered up so to say."

"We got a survivor over here," said one of the workers.

Everyone stopped what they were doing and ran to the edge. There was a figure crouched down in the middle of the debris in the hole. Clothes tattered and singed from the fire, but he knew who it was.

"McKenna!" yelled James.

He jumped into the hole and scrambled to her. There wasn't a lot left of the house, but it was just enough that he needed to be cautious. He climbed over some half smoldering beams until he reached her. He crouched down in front of her and placed his hand on her shoulder. She reached up with one of her hands and placed it on his. Slowly she stood up. He stood with her.

"Are you ok?" he asked trying to look at her through her matted hair hanging in her face.

"I am fine," she said. "We are all fine."

"We?"

She slowly lifted her head until she stared at him with her black eyes, face covered in blood and soot. She opened her mouth and black goo poured out. He screamed and tried to pull his hand away. Her grip was strong. She moved with lightning speed and brought his hand to her mouth.

"We are all fine," she said biting into his hand. He screamed, fighting her bite. He broke free and fell back to the ground. Screaming he saw his hand hanging from her mouth. She looked up at the others, raised her arm and pointed.

Creatures poured out of the hole, climbing the walls and dragging the men and women watching back down with them. Fighting to get back out, the men and women used anything they could find to climb on, only to be dragged back into the hole. They screamed as more creatures pounced on them, ripping their limbs from their bodies, biting and tearing at their flesh. Soon the creatures dragged their catch into the small hole McKenna had tried to escape in. Screams echoed from within as more creatures attacked them once they entered the large cavern at the end of the small hole. Last to climb through the hole was McKenna.

"We are all fine," she whispered before disappearing into the dark.

FOUR DAYS LATER

"Mystery still surrounds the disappearance of the entire Haunted House Debunkers investigation team, 2 sheriff's deputies and 6 construction workers from 4 nights ago. The Haunted House Debunkers had entered the old Michaels house to prove once and for all if the house was haunted and to hopefully find out what happened to some teenaged boys who disappeared there on Halloween.

One of the investigation team had come back into town that night asking for help. The report states that the team was trapped inside by some sort of devilish creatures. The fire department and sheriff's department responded to the request. Unfortunately, the house was engulfed in flames, making a rescue impossible.

Because of the intense heat from the house the fire chief and sheriff made the decision to allow the house to burn down to its foundation. They also hoped to stop any future missing person's reports from ever having to be filed because of the Michael's house. We are told it took several hours before the house was gone. There was a call from the site for a truck filled with dirt to smother the remaining embers and to fill in the large basement under the house.

According to the sheriff, this was the last time any of them were ever heard from. When a few deputies came out to check on why they weren't responding to radio calls. The vehicles were found but nothing else. As of today they are still searching," said the female reporter. "Though the search will need to be called off soon as the property has been sold and a new housing development will start building on the land within the next few weeks."

Four weeks from the news report, there still as no sign of any of them. The sheriff officially put the case into cold case status, hoping that the housing developers might put an end to the rumors. The new owner of the property took ownership and prepped the land for building.

The housing development, named Michael's Field, was complete in 18 months from the date they first broke ground. Houses sold faster than they could build them. Everyone wanted to own a piece of the Michael's property. The last house to be built was the one built on the original spot the Michael's house burned at. A new family relocating to Montana bought it and look forward to living there. They knew nothing of the history that surrounded the property. No one in town mentioned it either, they were just glad to see the house gone.

Epilogue:

Tap. Tap. Tap. Tap. It started every night. The consistent tapping that wouldn't let her sleep. It was loud enough to keep her awake all night long. Steady and constant.

Jenna always heard the tapping. Every night when she got ready for bed, climbed in and turned off the light, it started. At first she thought it was an animal in the walls, but pest control ruled that out. The house was brand new. There was no way they could have gotten in. Then she thought it was the shutters on the window, but they were screwed in and barely moved when she tried. Nothing in her room could make that noise. Most of her belongs were in boxes still. They had only moved in a few weeks ago and were the last to enter the new tract of homes.

When she was able to fall asleep, the tapping would get so loud it would wake her up. Playing her radio only worked so long before her parents would come in and turn it off. Once her parents closed her door the tapping would start up again. She even tried leaving her door open, but when she woke to the tapping, her door was closed.

She even tried to sleep on the couch, but the tapping followed her. Eventually she decided to wear headphones as her phone played music all night long. That found her some relief and she could sleep again. At least for a few days.

Except for tonight. Tonight when the tapping started, whatever was making the sound started shaking her bed. At first she thought it was a dream, but when she sat up and removed her headphones it did not stop. She felt the bed rocking front to back rhythmically. Peaking over the edge of the bed, she used the light from her phone to see. She started screaming

As her dad, Brad, ran into the room, the tapping and shaking got worse. He flipped on the light and stared at her. Then he saw why she was screaming. Grey, bony hands held the legs of the bed and shook while others tapped on the sides. He wasn't sure what he was seeing, but he knew that this was out of a nightmare. She tried to put her foot on the floor, but the tapping hands reached for her.

"Dad," Jenna yelled yanking her leg back onto the bed.

"Don't move," he said. He assessed the situation trying to find a solution.

"Stand up and jump to me," he said, taking a step towards the bed, just outside of reach of whatever was tapping her bed.

Standing with all the shaking was not easy, but she managed to do it. Her dad put out his arms to catch her. As she jumped, the bed moved. She landed too close to their reach, but managed to scurry away quickly. The door to her room slammed as they tried to run to it.

Soon the hands on the bed were hands with arms. Then the creatures came out. Black matted hair with grey skin covered skeleton bodies. Some black liquid poured slowly from their mouth, noses, ears and eyes. They crawled slowly towards them as they stood against the wall.

"What's going on?" said her mom from the other side of the door. She tried to open the door but it would not budge. "Open this door."

They ran to the door and tried to force it open. The creatures stood and walked slowly towards them. Her mom pushed on the door while they pulled. The door finally swung open, knocking them down.

"What the hell is going on in here?" her mom, Angie asked.

"Behind you," yelled Brad.

Her mom turned around and screamed. Brad and Jenna stood and scrambled again to the door. The creatures grabbed Angie and knocked her onto her face on the floor. Blood poured from her mouth and nose. They dragged her back towards the bed, she screamed and tried kicking them off. Brad grabbed her hands and tried to pull her back. Jenna joined him. Stepping out of the doorway, the door slammed again.

She ran back to the door, but again it would not open. Brad was fighting, trying get Angie from the creatures' grip. She grabbed the door knob to anchor herself.

"Dad," she yelled. "Take my hand."

She reached out and he grabbed her hand while still holding on to Angie. Together they fought hard to get her free. When her legs were under the bed, Brad lost his grip.

Angie tried to claw the ground to slow down whatever was that had her legs. She screamed and rolled onto her back. Dad crawled towards her but the creatures reached for him. He moved back to the door and tried to help open it.

Mom grabbed the side of the bed trying to keep the creatures from dragging her wherever under the bed they were taking her. She fought hard, pulling with all her strength on the side of Jenna's bed. Just when she thought she was going to break free, pain pierced through her body. She let go and screamed. Her forehead slammed against the side of the bed as she was finally dragged under.

As soon as Angie disappeared, the creatures followed. They could hear Angie screaming and yelling for help. Then there was nothing. No sound.

After a few minutes a hand covered in blood reached out from under the bed. It grabbed the side of the bed and pulled. It was Angie.

She slowly pulled herself from under the bed. Her head and body were covered with blood. She crept towards Jenna and her dad slowly, staying very close to the floor.

When she was about three feet away she stood. Standing in blood that pooled around her feet, she continued to stare at the floor. Her hair covered in blood and dripping covered her face, making it hard for them to see what she was thinking.

"Mom," said Jenna. "Are you ok?"

"I'm fine," she said. "We are all fine."

That was not her voice. Like something was talking through her. She slowly lifted up her head and looked at Jenna and Dad. They both screamed in terror.

Her face was covered in blood with black pouring from her mouth, nose, ears and eyes. Her eyes stared at them, but it wasn't her. Raising a hand she walked towards them. Creatures poured out from under the bed and rushed at them. Mom jumped on her father knocking Jenna to the floor. She threw him easily across the room, so hard he left a hole in the wall from his head. He slumped to the ground as she walked to him and lifted him with one hand. Angie looked at Jenna with look that sent cold shivers down her back. That was no longer her mother.

Biting a large chunk out of his neck, she spit it on the floor. Blood poured down his neck as he slowly slid down the bedroom wall. Jenna watched in terror as Mom lifted him again to drink the blood from his neck. She let him fall, walking towards Jenna as the creatures tore into Brad. When she was close, she crouched down to Jenna's level and crawled to her slowly.

"We're all fine now," she said as she reached for her. Jenna screamed.

20 minutes later

There was a knock on the front door.

"Who's there?" said Jenna.

"Stevensville Police," said a voice. "We got a call about screaming coming from here."

Jenna opened the door.

"We were watching a movie too loud," she apologized.

"Are your parents' home?" his partner asked. "We really need to talk to them."

"They're in the living room," she said. "Come in."

She stepped back to allow the officers inside. They walked to the back of the couch where Jenna's parents sat.

"Excuse me. We got a call about screams coming from this residence," said the first officer. "Is everything alright here?"

Mom stood with her back to the officers.

"We are fine," she answered.

She turned and looked at them. "We are all fine," she smiled, black goo pouring from her mouth.

The officers screamed and backed up. Creatures and Jenna attacked them as Mom and Dad jumped from the couch, knocking them to the ground. They tried to fire their guns and call for help. But the creatures were too fast.

THE END...for now.

Made in the USA
Middletown, DE
07 March 2023